CHICAGO WHITE SOX

ALL-TIME GREATS

BY TED COLEMAN

Book design by Jake Slavik
Cover design by Jake Slavik

Photographs ©: Charles Rex Arbogast/AP Images, cover (top), 1 (top); Jeff Roberson/AP Images, cover (bottom), 1 (bottom); Bain News Service/Library of Congress, 4, 7, 8; AP Images, 10, 12; Paul Shane/AP Images, 14; John Cordes/Icon Sportswire, 16; Ron LeBlanc/Icon Sportswire, 18; Scott W. Grau/Icon Sportswire, 20, 21

Press Box Books, an imprint of Press Room Editions.

ISBN
978-1-63494-502-8 (library bound)
978-1-63494-528-8 (paperback)
978-1-63494-578-3 (epub)
978-1-63494-554-7 (hosted ebook)

Library of Congress Control Number: 2022902470

Distributed by North Star Editions, Inc.
2297 Waters Drive
Mendota Heights, MN 55120
www.northstareditions.com

Printed in the United States of America
082022

ABOUT THE AUTHOR

Ted Coleman is a freelance sportswriter and children's book author who lives in Louisville, Kentucky, with his trusty Affenpinscher, Chloe.

TABLE OF CONTENTS

WHITE

CHAPTER 1

THE HITLESS WONDERS

The Chicago White Sox played for their first World Series title in 1906. It was just their sixth year in Major League Baseball (MLB). Those 1906 White Sox couldn't hit much. But they still managed to win lots of games. As a result, the Sox became known as the "the Hitless Wonders."

Fortunately, the team could count on pitcher **Doc White**. The lefty threw a great fastball. White started Game 6 of the 1906 World Series. He pitched all nine innings. And the Sox won the series. White's 159 career wins are still among the best in team history.

Pitcher **Ed Walsh** used his spitball to keep hitters off-balance. The pitch moved a lot in the air. But Walsh had great control over it. He became the ace of the 1906 White Sox. And in 1908, he won 40 games. Walsh still holds the team record for career earned run average (ERA).

The Hitless Wonders were long gone by 1917. By that time, second baseman **Eddie Collins** was one of the best hitters in baseball. In fact, Collins went on to record his 3,000th career hit with the

THE BLACK SOX

The White Sox returned to the World Series in 1919. Most people expected them to win easily. But they ended up losing to the Cincinnati Reds. Several members of the Sox had played poorly on purpose. Gamblers had paid the players to lose. It became known as the Black Sox Scandal. In response, MLB banned eight of the players from baseball. One of them was "Shoeless" Joe Jackson.

Sox. He was just the sixth player in MLB history to reach that mark.

Collins and outfielder **"Shoeless" Joe Jackson** rank first and second in Sox career batting average. Jackson's average of .356 is

fourth highest in MLB history. He and Collins led the White Sox to the 1917 World Series title.

The 1917 White Sox had some great pitchers, too. **Eddie Cicotte** was a master of the knuckleball. The pitch traveled slowly. But it danced in the air. That made it hard to hit.

Cicotte twice led the American League (AL) in wins.

Red Faber won three games in the 1917 World Series. He was a master of the spitball. It helped him post four 20-win seasons. MLB banned the spitball in 1920. But the league allowed Faber to keep using it until he retired in 1933.

Ted Lyons used a wide variety of pitches. Injuries made it hard for him to throw certain pitches. So he changed his style. That helped him play well into his 40s. Lyons retired in 1946. By then, the Sox were stuck in a long stretch without a World Series.

STAT SPOTLIGHT

CAREER WINS

WHITE SOX TEAM RECORD

Ted Lyons: 260

APPLING

4

CHAPTER 2

WORLD SERIES DROUGHT

The Chicago White Sox didn't reach the World Series from 1920 to 1958. But they still had plenty of great players to cheer for. Shortstop **Luke Appling** was a hitting machine. Appling had a great eye at the plate. He rarely struck out. And he racked up lots of walks. His batting average of .388 in 1936 was the best ever for a shortstop.

STAT SPOTLIGHT

CAREER HITS

WHITE SOX TEAM RECORD

Luke Appling: 2,749

Nellie Fox was even tougher to strike out than Appling. Fox struck out only 216 times in more than 10,000 plate appearances. He was also durable. Fox played nearly 800 games in a row at one point. He also had a great glove at second base.

Minnie Miñoso made history in 1951. The outfielder became the first Black player in White Sox history. He also turned out to be one of the greatest players in team history. "The Cuban Comet" was a regular Most Valuable Player (MVP) candidate.

Shortstop **Luis Aparicio** won Rookie of the Year in 1956. By 1959, "Little Louie" was runner-up for MVP. He also led the Sox to a World Series appearance that year. Aparicio made six All-Star teams during his 10 seasons with Chicago.

Billy Pierce dominated the mound during the 1950s. The lefty led the AL in ERA in 1955. Then he had back-to-back 20-win seasons in 1956 and 1957. Pierce spent 13 years with the White Sox. He recorded more strikeouts than any other pitcher in team history.

Pitcher **Wilbur Wood** was best known for his knuckleball. The pitch's slow speed didn't put much strain on Wood's arm. As a result, he started more than 40 games a season from

1971 to 1975. He once started both games of a doubleheader.

Catcher **Carlton Fisk** came to the White Sox in 1981. In 1983, he helped lead the team back to the postseason. Fisk was a great hitter. And his catching ability helped improve the Sox pitching staff.

Harold Baines came to Chicago around the same time as Fisk. Baines played in three different decades with the team. His last game with the Sox came in 2001. The slugger hit 221 home runs during his 14 years with the White Sox.

DICK ALLEN

Dick Allen played just three seasons with Chicago. But they were the best of his career. Allen made the All-Star team in all three seasons. He also earned MVP honors in 1972 as the Sox chased a postseason spot. Sox fans loved Allen for his towering home runs and helping the Sox win again.

THOMAS
35

CHAPTER 3

THE MODERN ERA

Fans called **Frank Thomas** "the Big Hurt." The name described the damage he could do to pitchers. During his first full season in 1991, Thomas smashed 32 home runs. The legend never stopped. Thomas won two MVP Awards. He also hit more homers than any other Sox player.

STAT SPOTLIGHT

CAREER HOME RUNS

WHITE SOX TEAM RECORD

Frank Thomas: 448

Teammate **Robin Ventura** provided his share of power, too. He also played expert defense at third base. Ventura won six Gold Glove Awards and hit nearly 200 homers. He later managed the Sox from 2012 to 2016.

For 12 seasons, pitcher **Mark Buehrle** was "Mr. Reliable" for the White Sox. Buehrle pitched more than 200 innings in all but his rookie season. Buehrle threw one no-hitter and one perfect game in a Sox uniform.

Paul Konerko formed a power-hitting duo with Thomas when he arrived in 1999. Konerko became just as much of a legend. He finished second behind Thomas in team career homers. Konerko was also a beloved teammate. He served as team captain. In 2005, he and Thomas led the Sox to their first World Series title in 88 years.

Chris Sale filled Buehrle's shoes as the next White Sox ace. Sale could throw his fastball more than 100 miles per hour. He started out as a reliever. But

OZZIE GUILLÉN

Ozzie Guillén was a three-time All-Star shortstop with the Sox. His teammates respected him, and he served as a captain. Those leadership skills helped Guillén manage the White Sox from 2004 to 2011. Guillén led them to their 2005 World Series title.

the team made him a starter in 2012. Then he became a regular All-Star. Sale averaged more strikeouts per nine innings than any other White Sox pitcher.

Chicago's next superstar arrived in 2014. **José Abreu** won Rookie of the Year that season. And in 2020, he was the league MVP.

Abreu stood out with his big power and big personality. He was a team leader for the Sox and a fan favorite.

Another fan favorite was shortstop **Tim Anderson**. Anderson played the game with style and loved having fun. More importantly, he was a great player. Anderson won the 2019 AL batting title and was an All-Star in 2021. Along with Abreu, he represented the next generation of White Sox greats.

TIMELINE

1901
DOC WHITE
(1903–13)
1910
EDDIE CICOTTE
(1912–20)
ED WALSH
(1904–16)
RED FABER
(1914–33)
"SHOELESS" JOE JACKSON
(1915–20)
1920
EDDIE COLLINS
(1915–26)
1930
TED LYONS
(1923–42, 1946)
LUKE APPLING
(1930–43, 1945–50)
1940
1950
BILLY PIERCE
(1949–61)
NELLIE FOX
(1950–63)
MINNIE MIÑOSO
(1951–57, 1960–61, 1964, 1976, 1980)
1960
LUIS APARICIO
(1956–62, 1968–70)
1970
WILBUR WOOD
(1967–78)
1980
HAROLD BAINES
(1980–89, 1996–97, 2000–01)
CARLTON FISK
(1981–93)
1990
ROBIN VENTURA
(1989–98)
PAUL KONERKO
(1999–2014)
FRANK THOMAS
(1990–2005)
2000
MARK BUEHRLE
(2000–11)
2010
CHRIS SALE
(2010–16)
TIM ANDERSON
(2016–)
JOSÉ ABREU
(2014–)
2020

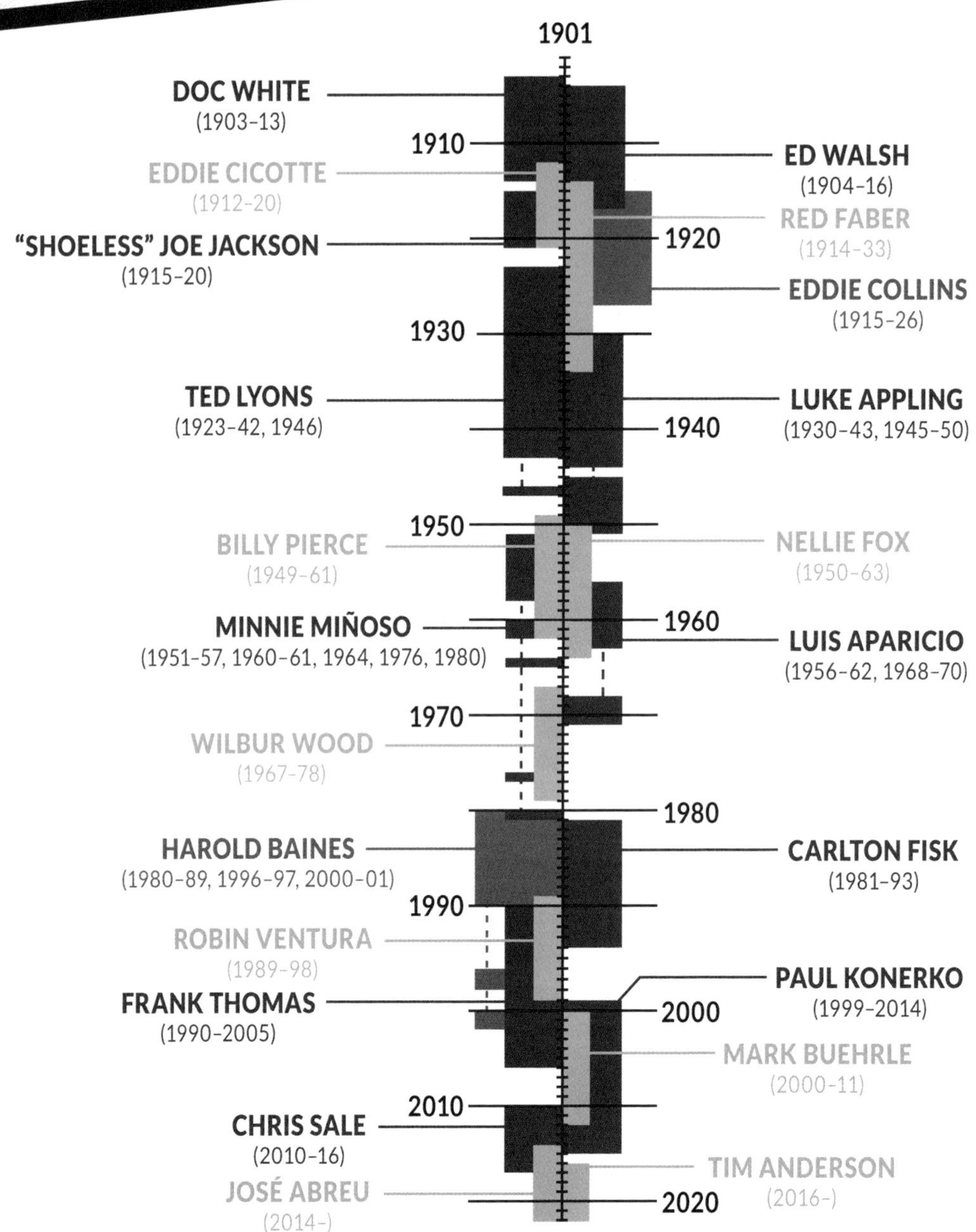

TEAM FACTS

CHICAGO WHITE SOX

Team history: Chicago White Stockings (1901–03), Chicago White Sox (1904–)

World Series titles: 3 (1906, 1917, 2005)*

Key managers:

Pants Rowland (1915–18)

339–247–4 (.578), 1 World Series title

Jimmy Dykes (1934–46)

899–940–11 (.489)

Al Lopez (1957–65, 1968–69)

840–650–5 (.564)

Ozzie Guillén (2004–11)

678–617 (.524), 1 World Series title

MORE INFORMATION

To learn more about the Chicago White Sox, go to **pressboxbooks.com/AllAccess**.

These links are routinely monitored and updated to provide the most current information available.

*through 2021

GLOSSARY

ace
The best starting pitcher on a team.

captain
A team's leader.

generation
A group of people who are all born around the same time.

no-hitter
A game in which a pitcher doesn't allow any hits.

perfect game
A game in which a pitcher doesn't allow any batters to reach base.

reliever
A pitcher who does not start the game.

rookie
A professional athlete in his or her first year of competition.

spitball
A now-illegal pitch that has spit or sweat on the ball to throw batters off.

INDEX